I0640581

Firebrand Firestorm

The Ancestors of Bjorn Esterday

Volume 12

Confrontation

July 2nd and 3rd 1776

Wynter Sommers

Wynter Sommers

USA Copyright © 2015 GJ dePillis
© 2015, TXu001966602 / 2015-05-08 and TXu001983965 / 2015-11-04

Library of Congress Control Number: 2020943167

Published by Pure Force Enterprises, Inc.
California, USA
Since 2002

INGRAM

INGRAM® Distribution

ISBN-13: 978-1-7184-0024-5
ISBN-10: 1-7184-0024-1

DEDICATION

To those who feel strongly about truth, justice, and the integrity of America; your honorable actions make us proud. To those who wonder if their daily choices matter; your small decisions impact generations to come. To those everyday people who don't think they have what it takes; when you strive for extraordinary things, the impossible becomes reality. Your dreams today become our future tomorrow. Thank you for everything you do.

Bjorn Esterday
Was Not Born Yesterday
Series

Firebrand (15 Volumes+Conversation Station Book)
Edges (9 Stories +Conversation Station Book)
Gone (18 Stories + Conversation Station Book)

Bjorn EDGES Series

EDGES Book 1-Swift Encounter
EDGES Book 2-Rousing Attack
EDGES Book 3-One Foot Under
EDGES Book 4-Earthshake
EDGES Book 5-Broken String
EDGES Book 6-Key Witness
EDGES Book 7-Who is She?
EDGES Book 8-Vanish
EDGES Book 9-Chase or Die

Bjorn Series Alternate Reading Plan

1st	Edges Book 1		22nd	Gone Book 10
2nd	Edges Book 2		23rd	Firebrand Vol 9
3rd	Gone Book 1		24rd	Gone Book 11
4th	Firebrand Vol 1		25th	Firebrand Vol 10
5th	Edges Book 3		26th	Gone Book 12
6th	Firebrand Vol 2		27th	Gone Book 13
7th	Gone Book 2		28th	Firebrand Vol 11
8th	Gone Book 3		29th	Gone Book 14
9th	Firebrand Vol 3		30th	Firebrand Vol 12
10th	Gone Book 4		31st	Gone Book 15
11th	Firebrand Vol 4		32nd	Firebrand Vol 13
12th	Gone Book 5		33rd	Gone Book 16
13th	Gone Book 6		34th	Firebrand Vol 14
14th	Edges Book 4		35th	Gone Book 17
15th	Firebrand Vol 5		36th	Firebrand Vol15 (End)
16th	Gone Book 7		37th	Gone Book 18 (End)
17th	Firebrand Vol 6		38th	Edges Book 5
18th	Gone Book 8		39th	Edges Book 6
19th	Firebrand Vol 7		40th	Edges Book 7
20th	Gone Book 9		41st	Edges Book 8
21st	Firebrand Vol 8		42nd	Edges Book 9(End)

ACKNOWLEDGMENTS

We acknowledge those who actively build peace. We acknowledge all the selfless talent which contributed to creating meaningful tokens of consideration and sharing. We acknowledge that every person has a daily choice of right or wrong... and we thank you for choosing the right, good, honorable path filled with integrity because that is the difficult and brave path. Small choices today become lasting monuments of loving hope tomorrow.

CONTENTS

0 PREFACE

After the foot-chase at the coffee shop, Bryce Aiden Tyler confronted Henry Mossop, the opera singer.

Now it is July 1776. It seems as if life is as uncertain in these colonies as ever... and to really shake things up, some people want to anger the King of England by proposing these colonies should be independent from the British Empire.

The ladies have headed to the docks to follow a concern that the ship must not sail. Meanwhile, Button is a captive. It seems as if Mossop will get away with his scheme, and Polly has her own issues to deal with, as does everyone. When trying to survive, how does one have the energy to think about the future of these disorganized colonies to form a united nation?

1 CHAPTER 114: (JULY 2 1776)
Watery Confrontation

Tweedbottom glared at Eliza and Jane while blinking rain out of his eyes while the ship pitched and yawed. Lightning cracked as the storm was now fully upon them.

Ignoring the rain, Jane boldly addressed Mr. Tweedbottom as they faced each other on the deck of the ship.

"You told me you were heading to New York for business, yet days later you remain in these colonies with a man in a sac?I cannot reconcile, Mr. Tweedbottom, that a fashionable gentleman with whom I've enjoyed tea is now pointing a weapon at me and is actually capable of kidnapping a man, who may very well be the husband of a friend of mine."

"Jane, my Darling..." Tweedbottom stumbled as the boat rocked. "It's not what you think..."

A blinding flash of lightning suddenly crashed across the ship with brilliant luminescence.

Eliza loosened her knees as the boat rocked, but the brief flare of lightning revealed something.

Eliza shouted at Jane, "We are not alone aboard, Jane... I saw something through the porthole in that door over there!"

Jane shouted at Tweedbottom, "Who else is aboard this vessel?"

Tweedbottom just replied, "Just the

cargo. Oh, Jane, I never meant for you to find out."

"Find out what? Are there other crew aboard?" Jane took a step closer to Mr. Tweedbottom as she pointed to the wheel, "Have you locked away the crew? Have you simply rigged that wheel with rope and wood, trusting that to navigate this vessel to your destination? On a night like this?"

"If I waited for Henry Mossop, I would have had to have to shared the profits," Mr. Tweedbottom explained with a whine.

Then a large wave curled up over the railing, slapping Mr. Tweedbottom, making him slip and stumble for balance. He dropped his firearm and it slid away from his grasp.

Eliza rushed to the door and looked inside the porthole, "Jane! He's locked up cargo, not crew."

"What?" Jane rushed over to Mr. Tweedbottom as he was temporarily

5

dazed. Jane quickly grabbed one of the many coils of rope strewn about the deck and bound Mr. Tweedbottom's hands.

Eliza called to Jane, again, "It's locked. Has he a key on his person?"

Jane patted the chest of Mr. Tweedbottom, but another crash of salty waves, left seaweed strewn across the deck of the unanchored vessel.

The sails, now not manned, were flapping about in a very disorganized manner. The roll of thunder rumbled as another crack emitted a streak of bright light from the ebony clouds and summoned wildly angry waves to crash onto the deck.

In a second strike, lighting hit the mast, igniting it into flames and shredding the sails as they glowed, then curled into ash and shrunk away with the beating winds. Seeing that Jane was struggling to grab onto something, Eliza took her firearm and aimed it at the lock, now opening the door. Inside the dark corridor, were more faces than she had imagined, all terrified.

Freezing water reached up over both sides of the ship pulling neatly coiled ropes and other debris into a tangled web across the deck.

Eliza called into the room, "If there is crew, we need you to take control of this vessel."

One voice called up from below, "The hull... Water is leaking in and we are all bound. Help!" Another smaller wave crashed. Jane now made her way SS to Eliza.

"They are bound. Have you a knife?" Eliza asked, "to cut their ropes?"

"The most frightening thing I anticipated today was sipping coffee for the first time while meeting Susanna Wright. I did not come prepared with a concealed knife nor did I bring a firearm. And before you ask, I could not find a key on Mr. Tweedbottom." Jane defended,

"Why not use your firearm?"

Eliza replied, "I didn't bring more than one wad of gunpowder and I've spent it on opening that door lock. Even if I had all my supplies, it is too rainy to reload..."

Eliza's hair was now matted to her face. She raised her wide skirts, now heavy with water, to see the water pooling around her feet. The boat rocked more violently, now.

Jane and Eliza looked at each other.

Helpless.

2 CHAPTER 115: (JULY 2 1776)
Magistrate Pinkney and Bryce
Searching Aimlessly

With Silversmith sitting at his side within the official carriage, Magistrate Pinkney, Mr. Bryce Aiden Tyler and the Magistrate's men raced to the docks.

A few of the Magistrate's uniformed men followed on horseback behind the official carriage. "No sensible sailor would sail in this storm," Bryce shouted through the pelting rain.

"We think it is Mr. Tweedbottom, the tailor, who is trying to sail," Silversmith added.

The horses rode onto the docks and halted right in front of the tethered boats and anchored ships. "Which vessel is it, Silversmith?" the Magistrate demanded.

Ignoring the rain, Silversmith jumped from the carriage and looked around at all the bobbing anchored sea-faring vessels.

There was a gap where the ship should have been. Confused, Silversmith shook her head uncertain how to respond.

The magistrate turned to one of his men and snapped, "Get this woman back to the inn, now."

With efficient obedience, one of the men on horseback rode to Silversmith, pulling her up to sit behind him in the saddle.

"But, Magistrate Pinkney," Silversmith

shouted as the man kept her on horseback.

"Look!" Bryce shouted as he pointed, "There is a woman waving at us..." and without finishing his sentence, he too alighted from the carriage and raced toward the shadowy figure.

Breathlessly, Susanna Wright called to Bryce Aiden Tyler with a desperate plea, "Please, Sir, help. I've got an injured man in there," Susanna pointed to the building in which Button still lay unconscious in the cart, but dry and out of the rain. Then she pointed to the water and continued, "And my dear friends have been whisked out there, Sir."

"Injured?" Bryce asked as he waved the Magistrate and the others to his location

Susanna then saw Silversmith and raced to her crying out, "Oh, Silversmith!" She called up to the soldier who had Silversmith on horseback.

"Where is Miss Jane, Miss Susanna?" Silversmith asked.

"No time! Get her to the inn before the storm increases!" The magistrate shouted as he slapped the rump of the horse and the red coat galloped off with Silversmith clinging to him, her eyes shut to keep out the wind and rain.

Bryce Aiden Tyler ran up to Susanna Wright, "You know Silversmith? She is the maid to my friend Jane Hargreaves. Do you know where Miss Hargreaves is?"

"I'm so sorry to say," Susanna Wright replied, "After Silversmith left the docks to fetch you... that ramp... to load cargo or passengers... that one floating there... dislodged and the ship is out at sea... with both Eliza and Jane. I couldn't stop it."

Bryce grabbed both of Susanna's shoulders forcing her to face him directly, "'Jane'? Do you mean Jane Hargreaves?"

The Magistrate summoned another of his men on horseback, "Get this woman to the inn!" he indicated Susanna Wright. A steed immediately approached.

Susanna turned to the Magistrate. "Let me remain, sir. I think I can be of help to you," Susanna pleaded, "if you seek to rescue those aboard that ship!" Susanna pointed urgently to show where the faint dark outline of a ship could be seen bobbing in the ocean not far from shore.

3 CHAPTER 116: (JULY 2 1776) Get These Men Some Help

"What can you tell me of this ship?" Bryce shouted his demand at Susanna Wright as they stood amongst the Magistrate's men on the rain pelted docks.

Susanna Wright continued, "All I can tell you is that I did not see sailors. I saw only Mr. Tweedbottom... Oh!"

"Yes?" Bryce asked.

Susanna replied as she ran to where

14

the ship had been docked, "As it drifted out to sea, I saw the name on the side of the vessel was SPY."

Rain whipped around the party and started to drift from vertical to horizontal as the winds beat stronger.

Susanna pointed out to sea to show Magistrate Pinkney and Bryce Aiden Tyler, "You can see the shadow of it there. It's not far from shore... can you see the S-P-Y painted on the side? That is the vessel, which holds my two dear friends, Jane and Eliza. Can you save them?"

Magistrate Pinkney summoned one of his men and ordered, "There is an injured man lying in a cart over there. Take him to town to have his wounds tended to. Rouse the doctor from his cozy fireplace and bring him here as I anticipate soon receiving more injured in need of his services."

"Yes, Sir." The obedient regimental red-coated soldier deftly observed his commanding officer's orders. The soldier's black boots splashed mud on his white britches as he held his black hat with one hand, while he raced to where the injured Button lay.

Magistrate Pinkney hurried to Bryce Aiden Tyler, "I hope this storm is not as strong as the Hurricane of Independence 26 from last September. It killed four thousand souls!"

Bryce replied, looking up, "I trust this storm will not be as destructive as Newfoundland's disaster. Hopefully, none will die tonight."

4 CHAPTER 117: (JULY 2 1776) Knife? Key? Truth?

The winds whipped the waves, which rocked the Spy, the ship on which Mr. Tweedbottom had assumed command. Salty, debris-filled waves of water lapped on deck as the wind tossed the vessel about as if it were a child's toy. The cloth in the sails had ripped away and now the ship had lost its navigational direction.

Jane pushed her wet hair from her brow. Her shoes slipped beneath her. She kept her knees slightly bent as to absorb the violent rocking of the deck.

17

Jane searched the dank darkness for lights of Meeting Town on the horizon. Jane had become disoriented. Meeting Town did not look far off, but would that matter if she this ship were to sink. Jane breathed in deeply and rhythmically to avoid being sea sick.

She clung to the side of the galley door of the ship to keep from slipping in the heavy rain. Jane looked for Eliza.

Eliza was at the door where the captives were held in shadows. One voice shouted up to Eliza.

"We are in shackles. Wooden shackles, not ropes!" a man's voice cried from the depths below.

"Jane!" Eliza shouted over the rain, "they don't have ropes. A knife is useless... they are in wooden shackles."

Jane replied, "Perhaps Mr. Tweedbottom felt it would be easier to make his existing slaves carve out wooden shackles for the newly incoming

Wynter Sommers

slaves instead of having to employ a blacksmith."

"How are we to open it if you didn't find a key on Mr. Tweedbottom?" Eliza asked. Jane looked into the dark depths and shouted, "Can you come up on deck. All of you?"

One man climbed up to the top and stuck is face into the rain and said, "This is as far as the length will allow us. He connected us all. He said if one tried to swim away, we would all drown."

He shoved his wrists out and showed the wooden shackles, the same fashion as the one Jane had seen earlier, which bound the feet and ankles of Button in the burlap sack. These shackles, however only appeared to be around the prisoner's wrists.

Jane examined them and commented, "Wooden shackles..." Eliza replied, "You need an ax, not a key..."

From below, there was a collective cry

19

and commotion. "What is happening?" Jane cried out.

A voice from below was laced with panic, "The water is rising. We are tangled and cannot see..."

"There must be a key!" Jane reasoned, "If Mr. Tweedbottom created this device, then he has a way to open it."

"Jane!" Eliza shouted, "Where is Mr. Tweedbottom?"

Jane looked around and called back, "I'll find him. Eliza you free these souls and make sure they don't drown down there."

"But," Eliza shouted after Jane as she slipped and slid away across the deck in search of Mr. Tweedbottom, "What if there is no key?"

Jane replied, "Then, I'll find another way to free them."

Eliza shouted down, "Can you come up on deck all together, then?"

Jane raced to the railing and spun around when she felt something in her back.

Mr. Tweedbottom, free of any ropes, had found his firearm and had it pointed right at Jane. He played with a key dangling from a string around his neck.

"Do you wish to free them with this?" Mr. Tweedbottom taunted as he smiled, "Jane. Selling them will make me secure for life. Women never seem to have a head for business. We can right this ship and get to market on time. Join me."

"Mr. Tweedbottom!" Jane exclaimed.

"Jane. I have such strong feelings for you," Mr. Tweedbottom breathed as he stepped toward her causing Jane to back up to the railing, her back to the churning ocean. The muzzle of the firearm, pointed at her belly.

Mr. Tweedbottom seethed as he spoke, "I am a romantic man. The tragic loss of love is a memory I will savor in years to come."

"Tragic loss of love? Me?" Jane batted pins of rain out of her eyes and smiled at Tweedbottom, speaking loudly over the slap of the ocean against the side of the craft, "Mr. Tweedbottom, perhaps we can dock in safe harbors, wait until the storm passes and discuss this over tea?"

"I cannot, Jane, lose even more money by losing my cargo," Tweedbottom growled.

"You mean," Jane forced a smile, "You owe a great many debts and need to pay them?"

"Oh, Jane. I don't need to pay anybody back for anything. Once I have the profits from the sale of those slaves, then I make my own rules." Mr. Tweedbottom breathed in the rain, relieved, welcoming the needle-like pelting of each drop as it hammered his upturned face, "I know I contrived to meet you to get to Floyd Hargreaves, but I found your company pleasant."

Jane replied, "I recall your tales of brutality when you were a discarded tailor's apprentice in Europe. You ventured to the Colonies to taste the freedom you were denied. Why then, would you sell your neighbors and deny them their freedom?"

"I have exquisite expensive tastes..." Mr. Tweedbottom shrugged.

Jane inched away as she tried logic, "But is it morally right, Mr. Tweedbottom, to force others into life of slavery in order to support your tastes for fashion, inventions, and parties? For voluntarily spending more than you earned?"

"In this business," Mr. Tweedbottom snorted, "you shout out the new rules loudly enough and others will follow you. It doesn't matter if it is right or wrong. What matters is profit and access to the monarchy to influence his law so that it supports my goal of attaining endless wealth!"

A brilliant flash of lightening startled Mr. Tweedbottom. Without thinking, Jane rushed toward Mr. Tweedbottom and yanked the key from around his neck, breaking the string which held it.

Jane tossed it toward Eliza, who was watching cautiously from a distance.

Although Jane and Eliza had only boarded the Spy ship to retrieve Button, now that they were faced with these other innocent Colonial souls, both felt a moral obligation to help prevent them all from drowning in a watery grave.

Rain soaked the splintered wood of the mast. Gusts ripped away shreds of sailcloth. One piece smacked Eliza in her bodice, winding her as if she had been struck with the force of an Olympic discus.

The mast started to groan and fracture, exposing the dry core of the wood. Then a smoldering ember rested on the splinter and a small flame ensued.

The key skidded across the turbulent deck and Eliza Lucas dove into a puddle to grab it. She froze a moment uncertain if she should help Jane or free the colonists from the rising churning waters in the compartment in which they were trapped.

5 CHAPTER 118: (JULY 2, 1776)
Tweedbottom confronts Jane

Aboard the slippery decks of the Spy, now with shredded sails, Mr. Tweedbottom stomped toward Jane and shouted above the howling winds, "It would have worked if Floyd Hargreaves hadn't tried to stop us. I know you loved him..."

Jane couldn't ascertain if Mr. Tweedbottom was angry or sad. It looked as he were crying, but any emotion leaking out of Mr. Tweedbottom's eye was quickly obliterated by the spray of

26

rain mingled with angry hisses of salt water.

What concerned Jane was that Mr. Tweedbottom didn't even acknowledge that Jane had taken his key and thrown it to Eliza. It was as if he didn't feel the snap of the cord pulling free from his neck... What thoughts could Mr. Tweedbottom be so preoccupied with that he would find the potential releasing of his lucrative cargo so secondary in importance?

"My uncle Floyd?" Jane asked. Suddenly, her mind recalled their conversation at tea. What did Mr. Tweedbottom say to her? Then, alert, she bravely faced Mr. Tweedbottom with determination.

Jane shouted firmly "At tea. You said you knew I loved Uncle Floyd. Loved. Only later did I hear the bang, which you denied. You knew Uncle Floyd was dead in the other room long before you even arrived for tea, didn't you?"

"Oh, Jane..." Mr. Tweedbottom started.

Jane continued, "Then, you read the invitation to Lady Sarah Wilson's party featuring that dreadful singer Henry Mossop and you used your monocle..."

"Jane..." Mr. Tweedbottom groaned.

"You," Jane's brow furrowed, "You needed my lorgnette to see the lace detail on the lithograph because you did NOT have your monocle during our tea, yet you did after Magistrate Pinkney, his brother and the doctor arrived. I know you need magnification to read as you used your monocle to read that poem I gave to you at Lady Sarah Wilson's."

"The demise of your uncle was simply business..." Mr. Tweedbottom continued, "Do you think I took any pleasure in deriving ways to keep your staff busy while I fulfilled my business obligation?"

Scoffing, Jane retorted, "Business obligation? Is that the new term for murder, Mr. Tweedbottom?"

Mr. Tweedbottom smiled, "The world is full of secrets one must keep to prove their loyalty to earn a profit."

"Loyalty to lies, wickedness... and murder?" Jane demanded.

Jane struggled for words as she felt the weight of her dress get heavier with the moisture her petticoats absorbed from the rain.

"Don't scold, Jane. It's very unlady-like. I loved our teas..." Tweedbottom shook his head as if he'd miss them in future.

"Yes. Tea. Loved the tea," Jane now realized she was in a vulnerable position and softened her tone of voice, "Let's continue to love having tea together. Let us plan another tea, shall we, Mr. Tweedbottom?" Jane's words tumbled out of her mouth in a rush. Jane held out a hand on the railing as she pushed her other palm toward Mr. Tweedbottom to keep an arms-length distance from her.

Jane blurted, "One week from Saturday. Would taking tea then be convenient for you, Mr. Tweedbottom? Perhaps you could go ashore and check your diary?"

Mr. Tweedbottom pushed aside Jane's arm and lowered his firearm. Jane relaxed, confident that she was getting through to him.

Mr. Tweedbottom became rather reflective as he pulled Jane closer to him and said, "Your uncle, Jane, should never had listened to the gossip spread by that Tallman Indian chap..." He sighed as he continued, "Fashions always change and the burden of creating something new which people will buy... it's too much. At least I know that people will always thirst for feeling more powerful by using other people...

"Slavery is in demand. It is a more stable and lucrative industry than fashions ever could be. Maybe one day, I can devise a plan to combine the two businesses I have grown to love..."

Jane forced a smile as she searched for Eliza, "Mr. Tweedbottom," Jane started.

Jane noticed the deck strewn with coiled and uncoiled ropes. Hundreds of yards of the stuff. This rope was probably used to secure large crates and haul them on board, Jane briefly reasoned. She noticed the section of railing she was gripping had a heavy hinge attached. She retained eye contact with Mr.Tweedbottom as she purposely stepped one foot into one coil and another foot into another coil to keep her from sliding around the slick rocking deck.

With a deep breath, Jane smiled at Mr. Tweedbottom and bluntly asked, "I must ask plainly, Mr. Tweedbottom... Did... you... kill my uncle Floyd?"

"With the honor of a gentleman. Yes, but it was simply for business reasons," He gave a quick nod.

The lightning cracked and waves tossed the ship around in a circle one way, then the other. Trunks and other objects, which had been on deck, now were bobbing around in the ocean far below as each retreating wave took more souvenirs from the vessel.

Jane's expression froze in a blaze of lightning.

All at once, feelings enveloped Jane as her face clouded with thoughts of betrayal, being too naïve, and overwhelming disgust.

She became angry with herself for having befriended a man, even encouraging his affections actively. She had encouraged a man who responded with such feigning outward adoration that she didn't take the time to evaluate his true motives.

She was so eager to have the social standing of wife, that she ignored any sign of ulterior motive.

He feigned devotion, but with cold heart, Mr. Tweedbottom had taken away her beloved Uncle Floyd with a smile. Uncle Floyd had welcomed Jane and Silversmith in when all others eschewed her after her parents died in England.

Jane was angry that she had sipped tea and chatted about the frivolities of lace and fashion with a man who knew her uncle lay dead in the other room. Her stomach knotted and mouth went dry. Her shoulders tensed and a pounding in her head increased.

Mr. Tweedbottom continued, "I was so fortunate to have met Henry Mossop and Lady Sarah Wilson. Mr. Mossop had a deal with a man in King George's treasury to capture anti-royalist colonists and sell them into slavery." He pushed Jane fully up against the railing as he continued, "I needed you as an excuse to get to Floyd and was pleased you started inviting me to tea. I kept your staff busy with one comment about lopsided skirts and I knew you had fallen in love with me. It was so easy to manipulate you, Jane." He took a breath and added, "That opera singer and the courtesan both taught me so much about how I can grab a life of freedom along with the luxury I am entitled to."

Jane smiled, realizing she had just been insulted, and threatened all at once.

"Can it be called freedom," Jane asked, "when you must sacrifice the freedom of others to attain it? Can it be considered entitled wealth, when it is wealth stolen from the profits of other's sufferings? Why not simply invent a new and better object, sell it and make a profit that way? Mr. Tweedbottom, it is never too late to change and pay for the sins committed. You are brilliant and can create..."

Mr. Tweedbottom shook his head, "That takes too long! Nobody gets rich unless they take it with force. Your uncle kept freeing people our Indians would kidnap. It was my idea to hire gold-seeking Indians to capture these colonists, take them to a ship, then to market for sale. I have a head for this sort of business. Now, I can set up my own venture. My own rules. "

The wind whipped around them, flattening Jane to the edge of the railing. Her hands slipped on the wet wood as she grappled for support. She kept her knees loose and avoided slipping by allowing her skirts to camouflage her feet being anchored—one leg each secure in its own coil of rope.

The boat pitched then yawed violently. A crack reverberated through the howling wind as a portion of the wooden structure broke free from the ship, and went crashing into the ocean.

Lighting blazed and struck another mast, setting it on fire. Another curtain of rain soon extinguished that fire, giving Jane a moment to think.

6 CHAPTER 119: (JULY 2, 1776) Eliza Makes a choice

Eliza rushed to the door, which held the prisoner slaves, but the wind had slammed it shut. She pounded on the door, shouting for the occupants to help push it open. They tried but the wind was too strong.

The wind jarred Mr. Tweedbottom and he staggered off balance as he came closer to Jane, with the muzzle of his firearm pointed at her belly.

"Indeed, Mr. Tweedbottom. Shrewd choice to have killed my uncle and made a deal with the King's treasury to continue your colonial slave trade. But, now that I know..." Jane wondered aloud.

Mr. Tweedbottom smiled as if pleased he could share his secret, "It is only fitting that you know the truth before you join your Uncle."

Eliza turned around and stepped toward Jane, hearing only snippets of the conversation being exchanged between Tweedbottom and Jane. Eliza heard enough to know that Mr. Tweedbottom was a confessed murderer. Eliza stepped toward Jane to see if she could help.

Jane saw her from over Mr. Tweedbottom's shoulder, coming up behind him.

"Oh, my. What a clever plan, Mr. Tweedbottom. Somehow making actual murder appear to be self- murder. Yet, if you are insinuating you wish to do away with me, might I point out," Jane started as she stared down at the muzzle in her ribs, then glanced back up at Mr. Tweedbottom, " ..a flaw in your plan. You see... a ball of lead in my abdomen would not... not... NOT look like self-murder, Mr. Tweedbottom... So, let us not speak of it again, agreed?"

Eliza stumbled and fell, the key spun from her grasp. She scrambled on hands and knees to try and find it. The wind filled her skirts and pushed her on her back, then with each gust, Eliza was pushed backwards as if her skirts were a sail. Eliza's head bumped against the edge of the opposite railing, back near the prisoner door.

Jane gasped in horror as she witnessed this from behind Tweedbottom's oblivious form.

"But," Mr. Tweedbottom muttered, now considering Jane's point, "You could accidentally and tragically become a casualty of this horrific storm, Jane," Mr. Tweedbottom retorted as if he actually had thought it out.

The boat tossed and turned. Another crack of lighting struck another tall mast.

Eliza, having mastered her wardrobe mishap, now saw the key glint with the reflections of the fiery sail above it.

She looked at Jane and Tweedbottom and then she looked at the prisoner door. The men inside had united forces and pushed the door open, yet they were still constrained. The water below was rising. Eliza scrambled through the flaming debris and grabbed the key, now searing hot, with her bare hands.

Eliza approached the first man and saw how all the wooden shackles were linked together. She went inside the tiny compartment, barely able to navigate past the pressed bodies, down the ladder, deeper into the water.

Mr. Tweedbottom shouted at Jane, "I think you should know the way I killed your Uncle, Jane. It actually took place much earlier. I locked the library door from the inside. I slipped out the window and then set up a pile of gun powder in the sun to fire some time during our tea. After I closed the window, did I realize I needed something to concentrate the energy of the afternoon sun to spark the gunpowder so I set up my monocle outside the window... but of course later I needed to retrieve it. You still ran to me for comfort. It was an easy matter to make that Bryce Aiden Tyler partner of your uncle's look guilty."

A monstrous wave crashed across the bow of the ship, drenching Eliza, forcing her to her knees.

She struggled to get up and pushed her hair from her face.

She glanced at the frightened wide-eyed captives, grasping at each other to keep their heads above water in the tiny cabin below deck.

Tweedbottom's betrayal had discretely shattered Jane's heart with the gentle swipe of a feather. Tweedbottom used his body to push Jane toward the railing, toward the yawning watery destiny beneath.

He reached around her and unlocked the hinge on the rail behind Jane.

Eliza was below deck, fighting the bubbling of her skirts to reach the chain and find the last man who was holding the lock above his head, willing to die to save the others. He was the last in line and would have been the first to drown, yet he held the lock overhead in hopes Eliza would come to the rescue.

Eliza did, holding the key firmly, refusing to release her grasp. Her waist was now under water, the salty water giving buoyancy to her skirts in the cramped quarters. His chin was now at water's edge and he was anchored so he could not float.

Eliza reached down and the key finally met the keyhole. Inside, the key slipped and Eliza turned it, tumbling open as plopped herself into the cold scratchy debris filled water.

The hand, which held the lock overhead disappeared for a moment, and then the full head of a man, gasping for air, broke the surface with a rush. The others felt the chains fall from them and they all scrambled out on deck.

From the watery slave cabin below deck, Eliza emerged like a captain insisting his crew disembark safely before he does.

This was not, however, Eliza's ship. Nor was she captain, yet Eliza Lucas felt a responsibility to these desperate souls. She felt relieved that Jane was still communicating with Mr. Tweedbottom, keeping him distracted as Eliza worked to free these people.

Eliza handed the key to one of them and they were able to fully unshackle each other. Some obviously had sailing expertise as they now disbursed and set to trying to gain control of the ship.

A frightful groan of the wood submitting to the pressure of nature's fury jolted the ship, causing all occupants on deck to slide to the opposite side. Eliza grabbed a flaming bit of splintered wood and crept up behind Mr. Tweedbottom, but Mr. Tweedbottom sensed Eliza's approach.

Jane glanced at Eliza fearing her eyes gave away Eliza's intention.

Jane kept her legs firmly planted in the coils of the ropes for balance as she helplessly saw Mr. Tweedbottom whip around to block Eliza's attack.

During this sudden movement, Mr. Tweedbottom's firearm discharged, but not into Jane, rather into a rolling barrel, which must have been filled with a combustible liquid.

As one of the embers languidly floated over to the viscous pool of oozing liquid, igniting it into a small flame, which danced about in the rain drops, but then... as if on stage and welcoming an audience, it blazed into a mighty fire. Mr. Tweedbottom fell to his knees.

Jane shouted to Eliza, "He was paid profits from slave sales!"

Eliza, flat on her stomach, clinging onto anything she could to keep from sliding about, struggled to her feet.

Tweedbottom shot back, "You have no head for business, Jane! The operation was funded by the King's treasury, which replenished its accounts by accusing Colonists of crimes. Then, we threatened them with either prison or all their money and assets."

"Is this all to fund the wars of King George?" Eliza shouted, trying to keep the conversation going to give Jane time to escape.

Mr. Tweedbottom actually answered Eliza, "War must be funded. My enterprise is patriotic, making the king's purse fat."

Jane now realized her feet had become entangled in the very coils of rope she had used to keep her steady, but now the ropes made it impossible for her to free herself from her position.

"Silversmith," Jane choked in the smoke from the flames, "said she observed your attitude as being contemptuous, critical, sometimes silent and unresponsive, then suddenly acting as if you were a victim defending against attack, looking for something to blame, to justify your actions, when it was you who was unleashing venomous commentary."

"Pity," Mr. Tweedbottom shook his head with a malicious smile, "you didn't listen, but you never do listen to anything... do you, Jane, else you wouldn't be here now, would you?"

Eliza raced to the other prisoners on deck to enlist their help in subduing Mr. Tweedbottom. These now freed colonists were very happy to oblige. They staggered and tumbled across the volatile ship's deck as they headed toward Jane and Mr. Tweedbottom, but the blazing barrel of oil now separated them as the flames rose like a curtain of heat and light, making the deck below them precarious and flimsy.

With the sting of smoke in their eyes, the silhouette of Mr. Tweedbottom and Jane became obscured.

The rain splashing about, the winds whipping around, the lightning searing into the waters and wood around them all made it impossible to get to Jane.

The fire took center stage, now as it spread like a curtain.

Jane coughed as she squinted into the black smoke. The needles of water pelting her face and neck made her wince.

Her ankle became twisted in the ropes and she slipped and fell backward as she tugged at the tangled coils around her ankles.

She saw the outline of people trying to breech the line of the fire to reach her, helpless to do anything as each gust of wind strengthened the wall of flames.

Once he had regained his balance, Mr. Tweedbottom laughed, as he reached down to Jane's ankles and freed her from the coils. With one arm and exaggerated strength, which shocked Jane, Mr. Tweedbottom pulled her back up to her feet, pulled her close, then pressed his lips against hers.

Mr. Tweedbottom said calmly, "Goodbye, Jane. I'll miss our teas..."

7 CHAPTER 120: (JULY 2 1776) Eliza Reached for Jane

As if in answer to Eliza Lucas' fervent prayers, a water soaked portion of the sailcloth above them tore away and fell on top of the wall of flames, extinguishing a portion of it.

Racing over, Eliza and the men behind her saw the glow from the flames cast eerie shadows onto Mr. Tweedbottom. He stood there, calm amongst the chaos. He appeared to be almost welcoming the surfer aromas, as if getting used to his home in the afterlife, filled with molten fires, sulfur, and eternal loneliness. For a moment, it was as if his face betrayed the core of his heart.

No longer was he the fashion obsessed man, eager to please the wealthy set at any price. Now, he was capable of so much more evil and greed. His change was slow and imperceptible. Now, he had come too far to go back.

Desire for more was his only motive, and he knew he would never be satisfied, always craving. Always yearning. Seeking brief moments of satisfaction when he could prove he was stronger than somebody else by forcing his will on them. His truly craven nature rose from his hidden soul up to the twisted contorted face which was the canvas for the dancing shadows, caused by the blaze around him.

One man sprinted through the pathway caused by the wet sailcloth and ripped off a chunk of wood as he dashed forward. He used the wood to push the oozing, burning barrel overboard. He ordered the others to rip down the remaining sails to try and extinguish the rest of the fire.

Additional men subdued Mr. Tweedbottom before Eliza rushed to him. Eliza looked left, then right.

She cautiously looked toward the end of the wall of fire.

Another portion of sailcloth was coming down, and it splashed out another section of flames. Eliza, heart racing, leaned over the railing looking down into the pitch-black waters. She examined each coil of rope with a glance and looked for trails, which might lead somewhere.

In reality, Eliza's hunt lasted mere moments, but to Eliza it felt as if it were an eternity.

With rage lacing her voice, she charged at Mr. Tweedbottom, "Where is Jane? What did you do with Jane?"

"She joined her Uncle," was all Tweedbottom said, grinning.

"You sacrificed Jane for this?" Eliza swept her arms around her to show this Mr. Tweedbottom the foolish destruction his impatient selfish desires for speedy riches and entitlement had caused.

It was as if he could not see the chunks of the ship's hull, now floating in the water.

It was if he had not noticed the skeleton of the masts with sailcloth torn away and strewn across the deck.

It was as if he didn't notice the angle of the vessel would indicate sinking would be imminent.

It was as if he could not hear the screams of the captives, now freed fighting, for their lives. Some had already jumped into the inky churning waters, seeking escape from the blazing decks. It was as if Mr. Tweedbottom had instantaneously gone insane.

8 CHAPTER 121: (JULY 2, 1776): Eliza Misses Jane...

Eliza Lucas slipped and slid around the entire perimeter of the ship, the Spy. It would surely sink. How would she stay afloat? Other prisoners, she noticed, were already in the waters, clinging to floating debris. When would this storm end?

Repeatedly, Eliza shouted out into the wind whipped ebony void, "Jane! Jane! Can you hear me?" Eliza listened, yet heard no reply.

Thunder rumbled. Lightning streaked across the ebony skies like a splash of molten silver.

"Do what you can," one freed captive said to the other. He pointed to Mr. Tweedbottom and said, "I'll put that slave trader where he daren't do us more harm. If we survive 'til morning, justice will be served ashore."

This former prisoner pulled Mr. Tweedbottom up and pushed him into the dark recesses of an enclave, wedging his unconscious form, there.

Then, the man sprinted to aid the other Colonists attempting to gain control of the vessel. With the helm damaged, they only wanted to keep most of it afloat until daybreak, when they could summon fishermen for help

Eliza glared at where Mr. Tweedbottom was stashed. Her stomach knotted with fear, knowing he had something to do with Jane's absence.

"Jane!" Eliza cried one last time. She paused. Listened. Nothing.

Nary two miles or less from shore, would they meet their demise so close to this land of Freedom? Would they ever again taste hot soup and fresh bread? Would these inky clouds demand souls sink to the floor of the ocean on this starless night?

Eliza, collapsed to her knees. Clinging to the railing, Eliza wrapped her shawl around the bars to anchor her. She saw dots of lights on the shores of Meeting Town, which she imagined emanated from crackling fireplaces. The horizon was obscured by her salty tears mingled with the cold salty water sprayed up from the black waters below, whipping her cheeks.

Hopeless.

It was all hopeless.

Suddenly the ship pitched steeply upward. A beam of wood dislodged from the structure and now threatened to slam into Eliza Lucas.

She scrambled out of the way as the log-like wood rolled off toward the railing, smashing into the cabin door along the way, revealing that the compartment in which the slaves had been contained, was now totally demolished.

Had Eliza saved them only to delay their deaths?

Eliza glanced over to where the man had stashed Mr. Tweedbottom, but now Mr. Tweedbottom was not there.

She craned her neck to peer about the ship, which now looked as if it had been fired upon by twenty cannons.

As Eliza moved, she realized her skirts were pinned down.

The whalebone hoops in the pannier under Eliza's skirt had provided barely enough resistance to keep the fallen debris from crushing her leg.

She was able to slip out from under the block of indiscernible wood and metal, which smashed a portion of her skirts flat to the deck.

She untied the ribbon around her waist and wiggled out of her bird cage underskirt, which had acted as a buffer, protecting her legs from being wounded in any way.

Once out of her skirts, Eliza Lucas tugged on her skirts, ripping away the corner which was trapped.

With the torn bit of cloth left in her hand, she wrapped her lower body in the scrap of fabric, which used to be her skirt.

Modesty was always rather paramount to Eliza Lucas. She could abandon her whalebone birdcage underskirts to return to the whales of the ocean.

Where, Eliza wondered, was Mr. Tweedbottom? Had he escaped to safety or was he killed at sea? Would they all succumb to a final watery fate?

She cried into the crook of her elbow as she clung to anything to anchor her as the others around her did.

The rain continued to whip across Eliza's face as she softly said, "Jane... Oh, Dear God in Heaven, bring Jane back to us... please..."

Eliza sobbed.

9 CHAPTER 122: (JULY 3 1776-1:00AM) The Doctor is In

Mrs. Dunlap raced out of Polly's guest room at the Meeting Town Inn and hurried down the staircase. She ignored the diners in the main room and rushed directly to the Innkeeper, who was just coming out of the kitchen.

In a panic, Mrs. Dunlap said, "Innkeeper, I must know where I can summon a physician or midwife!"

The Innkeeper looked at Mr. Dunlap and walked to a nearby table to rest a plate of food and pewter cup of ale in front of another guest. The Innkeeper glanced at the window and saw the rain pouring outside.

The Innkeeper replied, "You can ask the other guests, but it's a miserable night. I doubt anybody would come if summoned. Try again on the morrow."

Mrs. Dunlap insisted, "I really require somebody experienced in lady's matters straight away."

The Innkeeper shrugged and said, "No person is going to step out into that weather."

The Innkeeper pointed out the window and turned to Mrs. Dunlap, "You can see that blaze on the horizon? Out there? That's at the docks. Something is burning... and if we can see it over here, then it must be big. If a doctor is going outside, they'll tend to that mess, but not to anything in this cozy little Inn.

Wait 'til morning, Madame. You can have an ale free of charge. I'm sure that shall relieve your headache."

"It's not a head..." Mrs. Dunlap stopped, realizing no amount of logic was going to change the indifferent position of this Innkeeper. She certainly didn't want his filthy hands offering to touch Polly to bring a child into the world. She looked around at the guests eating and drinking. None of them were suitable for such a procedure. None of them.

Being uncharacteristically bold, Mrs. Dunlap raised her voice and asked, "Can anybody here direct me to a midwife?"

One patron, nursing a mead shouted , "Doctor Ale is here and he always keeps me happy."

Another woman laughed and added, "I'm a midwife... of love and my private consults are free!" then she winked at the man seated at the table a few feet away.

Another slurred, "Ain't Mr. Midwife in that shop with the dancing pig sign?"

Yet another boisterously laughed and corrected the first, "That ain't the Midwife, it's the butcher next to the doctor with the mermaid sign!"

The first woman joined in with a raucous laugh, "The mermaid maiden's shop? Where I get my cap and stockings and linen shifts to wear under me corset? You're a right help, you are!" The drunken patrons guffawed at their own jokes.

Frustrated, Mrs. Dunlap turned back to the Innkeeper who was tending to his guests. The innkeeper simply shrugged and walked back into the kitchen. Determined to make progress, Mrs. Dunlap turned toward the door of the Inn and marched to it, ignoring the jeers of the other patrons, still enjoying the afterglow of their own levity.

On the wall by the door were several pegs, on which patrons could hang their coats. Mrs. Dunlap grabbed one. She didn't know who it belonged to, but whoever the owner may have been, they were too drunk to notice Mrs. Dunlap taking it.

She'd return it once she was done, anyway.

She looked at all the patrons in the dining area and flung the cloak around her shoulders. Then, bracing for the windy streets outside, Mrs. Dunlap squinted and opened the door, closing it firmly behind her.

Now, which direction should she go?

10 CHAPTER 123: (JULY 3 1776-2:00AM) Determined Rescue

At the Meeting Town docks, Magistrate Karl Pinkney looked for Bryce Aiden Tyler, who had just learned from Susanna Wright that Jane Hargreaves was out at sea on the Spy ship. Not far from shore, they all helplessly watched as the masts on the ship blazed from the lightening and flames, which had ignited and now engulfed the vessel.

Bryce Aiden Tyler was determined to change the course of fate.

"Mr. Tyler... Mr. Tyler!" Magistrate Pinkney shouted through the wind and rain, "This is mad! Putting a small craft in those churning waters will be the death of you! The winds feel as if they gust to fifty knots."

Rain pelted down on Bryce as he ordered the Magistrate's men to help him secure a craft.

Bryce defended his plan by shouting his reply, "That ship is not far from shore, Magistrate Pinkney! I can reach them before they sink. And the winds have calmed. I'd wager to half the speed you just estimated."

"The rains may have decreased, but the lighting still flashes!" Magistrate Pinkney pointed to the blazing structure out at sea. "We all saw the lightning strike that ship," Magistrate Pinkney tried to reason through the cold pelting rain, "It will surely sink, even if the storm has weakened. Everybody aboard is already dead. We can wait over there for the storm to pass."

The Magistrate pointed to the building where Susanna Wright had tended to the constraints and wounds of Button before one of the Magistrate's men took Button into town to be treated to by the doctor in the village.

"And then what?" Bryce asked, "Merely count the bodies as they drift ashore?"

"Yes!" Magistrate Pinkney replied firmly, "We cannot risk adding to the bodies by having you go out to sea and dying."

Bryce Aiden Tyler noticed one of the Magistrate's men had selected a vessel and was untethering it. Bryce peered at the Magistrate. "Then you will not come with me?" Bryce asked.

"No! I will stay ashore." Magistrate Pinkney adamantly affirmed. He pointed to his men huddled to the side and added, "Should they suffer some mental ailment by assisting you in this risk-laden scheme? I should think that any of my men would concur that your proposal, sir, is sheer madness."

"Sir." Bryce smiled as he bowed to the Magistrate, then turned to his uniformed men and shouted, "Will any accompany me to try and find survivors of that ship ablaze out there?"

The men spoke briefly amongst themselves. Some stepped forward and others did not. Bryce looked to the Magistrate for direction.

The Magistrate shook his head and replied, "I expect all of you to return alive. Mr. Tyler is your captain, now." He leaned in toward Bryce and quietly said, "I shall pray God's hand is upon this foolish plan. It may be noble, but you may meet God this very night..."

Bryce nodded and then beckoned the men who agreed to assist him to board the small boat. He hurried to an immense coil of rope and then raced back to the Magistrate.

Bryce said, "That rope looks as if it has just arrived. Perhaps to be cut and sold to the sailors."

"Yes?" The Magistrate was confused.

"It may be long enough," Bryce commented, "To act as a main line to keep smaller row boats attached. This way, we can find our way back to shore. We are not going far. Could you simply guard it as it unspools? If we die, you can at least pull us all back to shore when the storm clears."

"Why try to rescue those whose fate is already sealed?" The Magistrate shouted. Bryce did not reply. The magistrate impatiently agreed to mind the rope.

Bryce grabbed the end of the rope and marched to his boat, where the men assigned to him were boarding.

Then Bryce Aiden Tyler snapped around, leaning into Magistrate Pinkney to hoarsely whisper, "Because if a physician told me that an untested procedure may save a patient who only had a ten percent chance of surviving...I would take it."

Bryce instructed his men, and each row boat slipped a smaller loop of rope over the main rope on the great spool. Then, Bryce joined his men in the larger wine-merchants boat to lead the way.

The wine merchants boat, captained by Bryce Aiden Tyler, along with the other smaller row boats behind him, all clung to the main rope as they disappeared into the furious storm ahead of them.

Their only guides were dancing flames flickering aboard the Spy ship encompassed by ebony brooding stormy skies, as broken masts and shredded sails sliced the winds with an eerie wail.

11 CHAPTER 124: (JULY 3 1776)
Oh, Hello

It was not long before Bryce Aiden Tyler, new captain of the small wine merchant's boat, and several of the Magistrate's men, who had volunteered to be sailors, were close to the Spy ship, which was ablaze.

The ship lurched upwards suddenly. Bryce reasoned perhaps somebody had dropped anchor to prevent it from being dragged even farther out to sea. This meant there were still survivors.

The clouds parted for a brief instant and something odd caught Bryce's eye.

There was a figure clinging to a rope, dangling off the side of the boat. The upwards lurch actually raised them higher above the water. The rope dangling off the side of the Spy appeared to have been kinked as a portion of it seemed stiff like a ladder rung.

And that person... were they upside down? Yes!

It appeared to be the rope had caught an ankle of the individual and their skirts were covering their face as she hung completely upside down and quite possibly was unconscious. The figure was tossed about in the wind like a wet bed sheet.

Then the clouds moved in to obscure the light of the moon and the only thing visible was the fire blazing on deck.

"Sir? I think there was a woman hanging off there." One man pointed to confirm what Bryce had just witnessed.

Bryce replied, "She obviously cannot climb up on deck into that fire and she cannot drop to the cold waters below. She would surely sink." Then he looked at all the men, "What have we aboard? Inventory!"

One man responded with "I saw barrels, glass bottles and corks down below." Another replied, "There is a whole wall of burlap sacks over there."

Bryce looked back to shore. The other rowboats, still tethered to the main line, were now clustering around the larger wine-merchant's boat.

They could all hear the cries of those aboard and the occasional splash as some either fell or jumped into the water.

Bryce issued his first order as captain of this commandeered vessel, "Take all the sacs and fill them with all the corks.

Tie each sealed cork-filled sac to the one long rope. Take all the barrels. Empty them. Stop them back up and toss them overboard."

A little confused, the men slowly headed toward their duties, hesitating.

"Quickly, fellows!" Bryce Aiden Tyler shouted. Then, the men executed these odd orders with haste. Bryce lit a small torch.

He leaned over the side of ship to be heard by the rowboats and issued this order, "Find any who are in the waters and pull them into your rowboats. Once full, direct the rest to cling to the barrels or these sacs, then you need to head back to shore to deposit the survivors and return to collect more."

The magistrate's men, whom Bryce Aiden Tyler commanded, were now throwing barrels over the side of the wine merchant's ship. The rowboats would have one man hang onto the barrels as the other man navigated toward the flaming vessel and searched for survivors in the water. Next, the men started tying the cork filled sacs onto a long rope and lowering each segment of rope into the water once it had something tied to it.

The Spy ship slapped down into the water, pushing a spray of icy saltwater to extinguish the torch Bryce held. As the Spy flopped back into the sea, the cascading ripples impacted the water, causing the smaller rowboats to lurch upward and splash down.

"Have we a lantern on board?" Bryce shouted to the men.

The clouds parted again, revealing the moonlight and Bryce saw the side of the ship once more... with the dangling rope, yet this time with no upside down woman tethered to it. The rope was now lax and flopped against the side of the ship like a cooked noodle.

12 CHAPTER 125: (JULY 3, 1776-4:00AM) The First Survivors Return to Docks

From the docks, Magistrate Pinkney nervously glanced at the anxious Susanna Wright. "Look! The first rowboat is approaching," The Magistrate announced.

"I'll see if Jane and Eliza are with your men, Magistrate Pinkney," Susanna said as she raced to where the boat was docking.

Magistrate Pinkney called out to

Susanna Wright, "Another is coming over this way." He called as he hurried to greet that boat and help survivors disembark.

The men who remained with Magistrate Pinkney, had gotten blankets for the survivors. The rain was now fading to a soft mist.

The first glow of dawn glimpsed over the horizon.

Methodically, the smaller rowboats unloaded survivors, and then returned to collect more. Hour after hour, more and more weary former colonial settlers who had been captured to be sold as slaves arrived at the dock. Finally, they had returned to the shores of their beloved land of freedom.

Susanna Wright searched amongst the survivors for her friends, Jane and Eliza. She still could not find her them.

Susanna greeted each shivering survivor with a warm blanket and instructed them where they might sit and rest.

Magistrate Pinkney asked his men, as they returned in their small rowboats, if all his other men were still well. They were. He was able to see each of the men who volunteered, yet he did not see Bryce Aiden Tyler.

Fishermen now appeared on the docks to evaluate the damage to their vessels and discuss if they could fish that day or not. Some offered assistance to the rescue efforts.

To Susanna's joy, finally one rowboat arrived with a very tattered Eliza Lucas. She was exhausted and her skirts torn, but she was alive.

Susanna Wright welcomed her with a warm blanket and as she wrapped Eliza's shoulders, Susanna searched for Jane Hargreaves.

"Where is Jane?" Susanna asked Eliza Lucas as she walked past Magistrate

Karl Pinkney. Susanna guided Eliza to where the other survivors were resting.

"Susanna," Eliza replied sadly, "Jane... Jane..." Eliza started haltingly, "The mast fell on top of Mr. Tweedbottom and it caused the boat to jut up nearly perpendicular, then it splashed down again. After that, I saw no sign of Mr. Tweedbottom."

"But what of Jane, Eliza?" Susanna pleaded.

Eliza avoided looking into Susanna's eyes, "Mr. Tweedbottom admitted to having thrown Jane overboard."

"Thrown overboard?" Susanna asked in disbelief. "To join her Uncle, he said." Eliza added.

Magistrate Pinkney overheard the conversation and he now added, "Join her uncle... as in..."

Eliza looked directly at the Magistrate and said, "I heard him admit to killing

77

Jane's Uncle Floyd. Making it look like Self-Murder, but was, in fact, murder." Eliza chocked on her words, tightly shut her eyes to prevent tears of frustration from greeting the world.

Suddenly anger welled up inside Eliza and she burst out with, "I know kid nabbing or stealing of children to provide a household with a servant has been happening to children for over a century... since the late 1600's, but look at all these survivors."

Eliza drew a measured breath before she hissed with defiance, "They are adults! Look at their clothes. They are folk of the middling trades. Yet, Mr. Tweedbottom hired Indians to wrest them from their homes? Why? To make people more afraid of the tribes than need be? To satisfy his debts? Why? What amount of profit could justify this!"

Eliza bit her lip as she looked at the survivors littered around the docks recovering from the ordeal, barely alive. With conflicting emotions, Eliza attempted to control her breathing as she drew the blanket Susanna had given her taut around her shoulders, shaking her head helplessly.

Susanna tried to comfort Eliza, but then Susanna noticed another rowboat approaching the docks loaded with newly rescued survivors.

While keeping her gaze locked on the incoming rowboat, Susanna Wright pushed Eliza Lucas into the arms of Magistrate Karl Pinkney, saying, "Magistrate Pinkney, please meet Miss Eliza Lucas."

She wove her way through the weary heaps of drenched survivors leaning against splintered boards, or laying on the ground succumbing to the sleep of utter exhaustion. Susanna Wright marched straight to the incoming rowboat exclaiming, "Have you pulled another woman from the waters? A woman named Jane? Dead or alive? Have you found Jane?"

The Magistrate looked out onto the water and then back at the matted wet Eliza Lucas now in his arms. His gaze wandered to the tenacious Susanna Wright, who was insistent that Jane be found.

The Magistrate shook his head. Bryce had not yet returned to shore.

Perhaps these souls were saved, but what of the life of his new friend, Bryce Aiden Tyler. Would all these survivors realize it was Bryce's insistence, which saved their lives? Would they appreciate that Bryce sacrificed his life for these people? For strangers?

"You must be brave, Miss Lucas," The Magistrate soothed awkwardly, "You were very brave and have helped save many souls."

"There is so much evil today..." Eliza Lucas mourned.

"As a woman of this New World, Miss Lucas," Magistrate Pinkney said, "You did not let evil flourish by ignoring it. Miss Wright explained how you rescued a man named Button... and you have also fostered the rescue of all these souls."

"But Jane... Jane..." Eliza started to cry.

Magistrate Karl Pinkney's voice cracked as he held this grief-stricken woman, "Your friend Jane.... I knew her briefly. Her friend... My friend, Mr. Bryce Aiden Tyler... I knew him well..." He cleared his throat, "Miss Lucas, we must remember them fondly for their sacrifices have shone the light of justice onto dark deeds. We must remember them."

He held Eliza Lucas just a little bit closer.

"Please call me Eliza," Eliza Lucas looked up into the Magistrate's misty eyes.

She cleared her throat as she bravely continued, fighting back tears, "I think to honor Jane, we should complete the investigation she started. She desired to prove her uncle was murdered and to bring the culprit to justice. She desired justice. We need to change this country so all people can receive equal and fair justice."

Eliza tightly pulled her scratchy blanket around her, as if to make herself smaller.

Sand and saltwater caused the boning of her corset to chafe her skin and she was very uncomfortable, but she was tormented by the thought of Jane's fate being worse than her own, and kept her complaints of discomfort to herself.

13 CHAPTER 126: (JULY 3, 1776) Turn Coats Turn. Susanna Dashes Off...

Susanna turned away from the docked rowboat, which did not contain Jane Hargreaves nor Bryce Aiden Tyler. She marched back to where Magistrate Pinkney and Eliza Lucas stood.

She observed the red uniformed jacket worn by Magistrate Pinkney and Susanna Wright said, "That crimson jacket..." She shook her head.

83

"Miss Wright?" Magistrate Pinkney asked with a quizzical look as he stepped away from Eliza Lucas.

"His Majesty," Susanna shared, "Wants to dishearten and discourage the exodus from England to these rugged shores by snatching back colonists who have left and he is punishing them by enslaving them."

"These people," The Magistrate replied, "All have a second chance at life."

Eliza joined in, "Mr. Tweedbottom sold his neighbor into slavery because he was enslaved by his own passions."

Susanna Wright added, "I believe Henry Mossop justified slavery to secure assistance from other lands to help tame these unruly terrains. This is why we need a land of rules and laws which encourage the best of our natures, not legally permit the vices which bring out our worst traits."

"According to Henry Mossop," The Magistrate commented, "Your Mr. Tweedbottom was in debt and it was easy for Mr. Tweedbottom and Mr. Mossop to justify their actions by telling themselves betraying their neighbors was helping His Majesty's cause. Such a complex twisted contradiction and certainly a door to insanity."

Eliza shook her head, "Oh, I assure you, Magistrate Pinkney that Mr. Tweedbottom hurled himself into insanity by insisting his actions of enslaving others would free him, when in reality, the guilt drove him mad. "

Susanna Wright added, "And poor Button is an example. He was a victim of those men using Indians to spread fear amongst the colonies where it is not warranted, all for the profits of blood soaked funds. But, that is why things need to change."

Susanna pointed a finger at the Magistrate's red jacket, "Those who sacrifice to voyage here, do not want His

Indulgent Majesty to whisk away their sons to forcibly serve in the King's Navy. Those who make this new place a home must know the local Indians have often welcomed and helped us. Despite the greed of some back in England who have made dishonorable deals by paying a small group of tribes to terrorize us, we know this land can become a land of freedom and equal justice for us all."

Eliza added, "No longer do they want to be denied medicine for sick families because they cannot afford to employ their own physician. No longer do they wish to pay for inferior imports when they can make better quality goods exactly here, on this soil..."

Surprising both Eliza and Susanna, Magistrate Pinkney added, "And they no longer wish for their brothers to be accused of crimes just so they are forced to liquidate their assets to send to the King's Treasury only to later discover that those monies then support the enslavement of middling colonists."

Turning to Magistrate Karl Pinkney, Eliza Lucas gently said, "If you ever discard that red Jacket, I happen to make a lovely indigo blue dye, which would quite compliment your complexion, Sir."

Susanna looked up suddenly. "Laws! I completely forgot!" She turned to Magistrate Pinkney, "Sir, may I please borrow..." Then she turned to Eliza as if her thoughts were racing faster than her mouth could utter words, "Eliza, you rest here. Stay safe."

With a wave of his hand, Magistrate Pinkney pointed to one of his men and stated, "Provide Miss Wright with whatever she requires... and has anybody seen any sign of the Wine Merchant's boat being captained by Bryce?"

14 CHAPTER 127: (JULY 4, 1776)
Silversmith Recruited

Streams of morning sunrise crested the horizon, silhouetting Susanna Wright clinging the waist of the red-coated soldier, which the Magistrate had appointed to be Susanna's chauffeur as they bolted into town on horseback.

"I may need to hire a carriage," Susanna shouted in the red-coat's ear as the horse galloped rhythmically.

"The Innkeeper can arrange one for you. I must return to my Magistrate to help, Miss Wright," the soldier yelled in reply, as a bit of saliva escaped his lips and hit Susanna in the eye. She did not dare to release her grip to tend to her eye, so instead squashed her eyes shut and swiped her face on the back of his crimson jacket.

When the steed halted in front of the Inn, Susanna slipped off, pushing her hand onto her thigh to prevent her skirts from revealing too much leg. Once her feet touched the ground, Susanna was confident her modesty was intact.

"I'll be back at the docks. Godspeed." The red-coated chauffeur assured.

Susanna smiled and thanked the soldier as she watched him ride off in the direction from which they had just come.

Realizing her appearance was in a state of disarray, Susanna boldly marched into the Inn ignoring any looks from early breakfasting guests, who might have commented on her unkempt appearance.

A moment later, Susanna was pounding on a bedroom door in the Inn. "Silversmith. Silversmith!" Susanna called through the door.

The door opened, "Miss Wright!" Silversmith uttered in surprise. Silversmith, always in the habit of raising early, was already dressed.

Susanna boldly strode into the guest room and closed the door behind her, looking very stern. "Silversmith," Susanna started, "I..."

Silversmith politely held a finger up to her lips, to indicate Susanna Wright should be silent.

Whispering, Susanna looked at Silversmith out of the corner of her eye, "Why must I be silent, Silversmith?"

In hushed tones, Silversmith explained as she tip toed to the Inn door, opened it, stepped into the hallway beckoning Susanna Wright to follow her. When she did, Silversmith quietly closed the door behind her.

In the hallway, Silversmith explained, "The storm last night made travels rough."

"You have no idea what rough..." Susanna started, indicating her own skewed appearance with a sweeping gesture.

Silversmith continued in a whisper, "They put all the servants into one room. MY room... to sleep. I chose to remain dressed all night lest one of the other servants took my dress either by accident or with thieving intentions. I do not wish to wake them with any news you may have. Miss Jane is rather particular about keeping confidences and I haven't checked yet to see if Miss Jane returned to her room."

Susanna took a deep breath, "Yes. Um... Jane... about Jane, Silversmith."

Susanna inhaled again before continuing softly to move away from the door into the hallway..."Silversmith, your mistress Jane... Silversmith..."

"Yes, Miss Susanna?" Silversmith urged.

Susanna Wright started again uncertain if she should tell Silversmith at this very moment as the shock may distress her terribly, "Mistress Jane's... whereabouts... are...."

"Oh, she must be chilled to the bone. She often takes early morning walks." Silversmith offered, "I can get her cloak and perhaps the kitchen would permit me some food to take to her."

Susanna Wright pushed her matted dusty tangled hair from out of her eyes and looked firmly at Silversmith, speaking very deliberately and earnestly.

"You won't need to bother the Innkeeper, Silversmith. You see..." Susanna struggled with how to continue,

"I was expecting a document to arrive and I wasn't here to meet the person who was to deliver it... Your Miss Jane..." and Susanna choked once more on her words.

Silversmith thought she understood and lowered her voice into a whisper causing Susanna Wright to lean in, "Remember when Miss Jane sent me to retrieve Mr. Tyler and Magistrate Pinkney and I returned them to the docks?"

She nodded.

Silversmith continued, saying, "Well, as you know, we had barely arrived, when Magistrate Pinkney assigned a man to take me immediately back to this Inn. Good thing, as it turns out, because I discovered from the Innkeeper himself that Mrs. Dunlap and Polly, both friends of Miss Jane had just arrived at the Inn. He had to turn away other travelers. They could have been the same ones you spoke with at the docks, that sailor from Ireland. The Innkeeper told me he had to turn most of them away. And wouldn't you know it? Mrs. Dunlap took pity on them for having taken the last rooms and she actually loaned them her carriage."

"Mrs. Dunlap, the printer's wife?" Susanna prodded anxiously, "She's arrived? Oh, that is good news. That is the person I was to meet! She has the documents!"

"But last night," Silversmith continued sadly, "Mrs. Dunlap bolted away at the height of the storm. I was told some patrons were laughing at how Mrs. Dunlap snatched up somebody's cloak and left."

"Left? On foot? Has she returned?" Susanna pleaded.

"Yes. On foot. She did not have her carriage, you see... she had just given it away to the very people we met at the docks... the ones you directed to this very Inn, Miss Wright," Silversmith shrugged. "But, we could ask Polly, perhaps. Her room is just down there."

Susanna whispered, "The Continental Congress is meeting today, Silversmith"

Susanna glanced furtively then locked her gaze as she continued, "Today is our only chance to make sure that document is accepted and signed. I'm sure Robert Livingston has brought one with him, but I need that copy. I tell you matters have become frightfully complicated and I have learned from past meetings that I must have a reserve plan to execute should the original plan fail... which it has on several occasions"

She clenched a fist to make a point and said firmly, "We need those men to commit to their ideas by signing their names in ink, committing to the concepts we have discussed in those meetings. Silversmith..." Susanna punctuated with a stern expression, "I need your help."

15 CHAPTER 128: (JULY 4, 1776)
Susanna Almost Tells Silversmith,
who fetches Billy

The early morning light fell on the storm battered sign of the Meeting Town Inn.

Only one remaining link of a chain kept the Inn's sign attached to the bar on which it had hung the day before.

Now, swinging precariously in the early morning breeze, the sign squeaked. Silversmith pitied the pedestrian who would unknowingly stand beneath that sign at just the wrong time only to have the wooden plaque fall upon their heads.

Susanna told Silversmith, "First, I need a carriage. I know you just said Mrs. Dunlap gave hers away, but…"

"Billy Dawes," Silversmith suggested, "Miss Jane's driver. He slept in the stables behind the Inn. He guards his horses so nobody takes them or his carriage."

Silversmith's eyes widened as she continued, "Oh, Billy Dawes is brilliant navigating muddy streets with tree branches and all matter of debris. Swift, he is. I assure you, I have ridden with him. Shall I check and see if I can rouse Billy Dawes and have him ready his carriage?"

"By all means," Susanna Wright replied, "I require one carriage and one driver. After this storm, both shall be difficult to come by."

"Before I dash to the stables, Miss Susanna... Please wait there..." Silversmith quietly slipped back into the guest room and out again in mere seconds. In her hand, she held a hairbrush, ribbon and a clean skirt from Jane's luggage and Jane's cloak. Silently, she offered it to Susanna Wright.

"Are these Jane's things?" Susanna Wright asked simply.

"You can return them to Miss Jane when you see her next. She won't mind," Silversmith responded. Looking at the items in her hand, Susanna accepted them tenderly, then looked at Silversmith.

Susanna's voice cracked as she said, "Thank you, Silversmith... please..."

Susanna flung the clean cloak over her own shoulders to hide Susanna's wrinkled, dirty dress.

The skirt, Susanna rolled up and tucked under her arm. Susanna thought if she met up with Eliza Lucas, she might need a change of skirt since hers was torn from the recent rescue.

Susanna laid down the hair brush and ribbon on a nearby ledge and slipped her hand into the slit of her skirts at her hip, into one of the small Pannier baskets, which provided the foundation of her skirts and also served as a pocket.

Susanna retrieved a small scrap of paper and showed it to Silversmith.

Susanna took a deep breath, then spoke, "Before you go, I am in need of your assistance, Miss Silversmith, to recognize the names on this list. Your mistress did teach you to read, correct?"

"Oh yes, Miss Wright, but..." Silversmith replied as she read the names on the list, nodding that she recognized some of them, "I met Mr. Peter Timothy earlier and I was outside your barn meeting just before it was raided. But, you would also know these men, would you not, Miss Susanna?

Weren't they at your barn meeting?"

"Yes," Susanna nodded, "But I may need to *Divide et impera.*"

"Pardon?" Silversmith scrunched up her nose, "I didn't understand what you just said..."

"Oh, it's a bit of philosophy from Philip the second, King of Macedon. It was penned from three centuries before Christ our Savior was born. Some say Julius Ceaser said it first, but... who can say for certain? The phrase means breaking up a larger mass into smaller more manageable ones. As women, we cannot approach all these men together, yet might be able to one at a time."

"Oh!" Silversmith nodded, "Divide and conquer. Well, if I fetch Billy, we'll have three heads to divide that list instead of just two."

"And," Susanna continued in a deliberate whisper, "You'll need to help me guard Mrs. Dunlap's document... the one to be signed... Although you are a servant, Silversmith, we are both standing in the land of choice. So, I present you with the option. Will you join me or will you remain here?"

Silversmith now pondered the question. "Signing that document will allow Miss Jane to complete her deceased Uncle Floyd's path. The one where he wanted to stop attacks on people like Polly and her husband. Stop snatching Colonists and enslaving them, that is... will it not?"

Susanna Wright nodded solemnly, "But, the path has not been easy, and it may very well get even more... uh... challenging, Silversmith."

Silversmith smiled and whispered, "Seems to me that the sooner I help you, the sooner we can all resume our plans to return home. Miss Jane would be pleased. Let me fetch Billy, then I can see if Polly has that document and if Mrs. Dunlap has returned... and after that, I would be happy to accompany you, Miss Susanna. I'll ask Billy to bring the carriage to the front of the Inn. Then, we shall all *Divide et impera...*"

"I shall wait out front, then," Susanna nodded. "It's a good plan, Silversmith."

As Silversmith scampered away, Susanna Wright realized she had not yet told Silversmith that Jane was thrown overboard and Eliza Lucas had witnessed it. Jane had died in the angry waters of that storm... and Mr. Bryce Aiden Tyler was also lost at sea.

She shook her head, sighing as she reached for the hairbrush. The bristles of Jane's hairbrush against Susanna's scalp shot a tingle from her neck to the base of her spine. Susanna wondered if all the effort and sacrifice to get this document signed was worth it. Would the results be lasting or simply be ignored?

Silversmith was Jane's lady's maid, cook, investigator, scribe, and whatever else Jane needed. This loyal companion remained at Jane Hargreaves' side as

Jane lost her fortune, lost her uncle, and now... lost her life. When would Susanna be brave enough to inform Silversmith Jane had just died at sea? How could she have hidden like a coward behind explaining some idiom instead of boldly stating the facts, which Silversmith had a right to know?

Susanna exhaled as she slowly picked up the ribbon to tie up her hair. Susanna wondered if Silversmith was a fragile raw egg, which might be crushed by the news that her mistress was now deceased. Then again, eggs are constructed to withstand quite a bit of pressure... such was God's design.

"Jane would have wanted us to press on..." Susanna said to herself as she now hurried to the front of the Inn to await the carriage.

16 What Just Happened?

After confronting the fear of water, Jane tumbles overboard. Meanwhile, although Bryce convinced Magistrate Pinkney to join him, they feel as if their searches are fruitless and aimless, but Bryce is determined to find the truth. .

Meanwhile, Mr. Tweedbottom has a frank discussion with Jane and she decides that this man should not be a marriage prospect for her... not now and not ever as his character lacks the discipline of a true polished gentleman.

Eliza Lucas' concerns are also stretched

as all her skills and talents must be used to make an inch of progress, but her hopes were dashed when she reached out to save Jane only to have her friend slip away into the watery depths...

After the storm, Eliza helps with the survivors, but she soon realizes Jane is not among those who were rescued.

As Eliza works, she thinks back to her friends struggling for freedom. They must overcome their personal griefs in order to pursue this concept. But how will they confront the King of England and ask for Colonial Independence. The price they have paid has been so great, they feel as if they have nothing left to lose.

17 Did You Know...

In Chapter 7 of Volume 7 in the *Firebrand* series, Mrs. Elizabeth Timothy's son, Peter, explains that his mother died in 1757, nearly twenty years prior to the day Silversmith and Billy strode into the bookshop.

Mrs Timothy had written a book. In those days, even though Mrs. Timothy owned a print shop and owned the Southern Carolina Gazette Newspaper (from 1737–1746); there were some topics she, as a respected lady, could not print. Some say that her friend Benjamin Franklin helped her publish a booklet on marriage advice .

So, when Billy Dawes simply grabbed a random book, he was unaware that it was the controversial book written by Elizabeth Timothy titled **"Reflections on Courtship and Marriage'** (The full text will be replicated   at the end of *Firebrand* Volume 15)

Although Billy Dawes and Silversmith are created fictional characters, there really was an Elizabeth Timothy. She was born in the Netherlands and moved to Philadelphia in 1731 and then South Carolina in 1733. She married Lewis Timothy and was widowed in December 1738. She was the first woman in America to publish a newspaper

Benjamin Franklin noted that Elizabeth Timothy had *"manag'd the Business with such Success that she not only brought up reputably a Family of Children, but at the Expiration of the Term was able to purchase of me the Printing House and establish her Son in it."*

The children of Elizabeth Timothy:

✓ Peter (c. 1725–1782);

✓ Louisa (Mrs.James Richards);

✓ Charles (d. September 1739);

✓ Mary Elizabeth (Mrs. Abraham Bourquin);

✓ Joseph (d. October 1739);

✓ Catherine (Mrs. Theodore Trezevant).

18 Vocabulary

In the early 1770s, before the colonies came together into the United States of America, some words and terms were used, which may be explained in this section.

Alight / Alighted: To step down from something high such as a carriage. To dismount from a horse.

Debris: Something torn or broken which is scattered around.

Divide et impera: This means "divide and conquer". This is a political strategy to cause conflict within your opponent's group in order to weaken them. When you successfully divide the strength of your opponent, when they are fighting among themselves, then it will be much easier to conquer them...

Emit / Emitted: Give out a sound, or liquid, or heat, or light.

Fashionable: Wearing clothes, doing things, going places that are popular at a particular time.

Luminescence: Light shining at a low temperature via chemical changes.

Reconcile: To be friends again. To find a way for two opposite ideas to agree.

Rig / Rigged: Placement of sails and masts of a ship.

Tether / Tethered: A rope or chain used for keeping an animal restrained.

Whine: To make a high, unhappy cry or sound.

:

ABOUT Wynter Sommers

Wynter Sommers is the pseudonym for an American writing team, which harnesses multiple skills in technology, research, history and education. Formally trained with a PhD in Education, Wynter Sommers blends academic classroom experience, with corporate sophistication, and a passion for developing more effective student insights through engaging storytelling.

Wynter Sommers has a heart to inspire creativity and develop critical thinking skills, all to encourage readers to make wise choices in life.

Wynter Sommers takes each story and weaves the plot with classic gripping elements, which endure throughout repeated readings, revealing new meanings each time the story is explored. The small choices a reader makes in real life could have a lasting effect in future generations. This set of stories shows the origin of not just Bjorn Esterday and Sarah Paradise, but of their ancestors and the sort of world which was established, which unfolded in each generation until Bjorn and Sarah met.

It is rewarding to learn of heartfelt, thought provoking conversations taking place globally about the characters of these books. Should the reader be presented with extraordinary circumstances, it is the sincerest wish that they act with honor, truth and integrity to overcome obstacles in real life whilst the reader hones skills of self-reliance and collaborative teamwork despite barriers outside of the reader's control. Wynter Sommers hopes you enjoy the other *Bjorn Esterday Was not Born Yesterday* stories in this series.

111